CRUMBS!

BEN BAILEY SMITH

ILLUSTRATED BY SAV AKYÜZ

BLOOMSBURY EDUCATION

BLOOMSBURY EDUCATION
Bloomsbury Publishing Plc
50 Bedford Square, London, WC1B 3DP, UK

BLOOMSBURY, BLOOMSBURY EDUCATION and the Diana logo
are trademarks of Bloomsbury Publishing Plc

First published in Great Britain in 2020 by Bloomsbury Publishing Plc

A catalogue record for this book is available from the British Library

ISBN: PB: 978-1-4729-7268-2; ePDF: 978-1-4729-7269-9; ePub: 978-1-4729-7266-8;
enhanced ePub: 978-1-4729-7265-1

2 4 6 8 10 9 7 5 3 1

Printed and bound in India by Replika Press Pvt. Ltd.

Old Farmer Dan was a hard-working man
But not quite the brightest you've seen.
His wife Kay was smart, his dog held
his heart;
They really were kind of a team.

One day at lunch,
Dan had a hunch
It might just be time
for a bite.

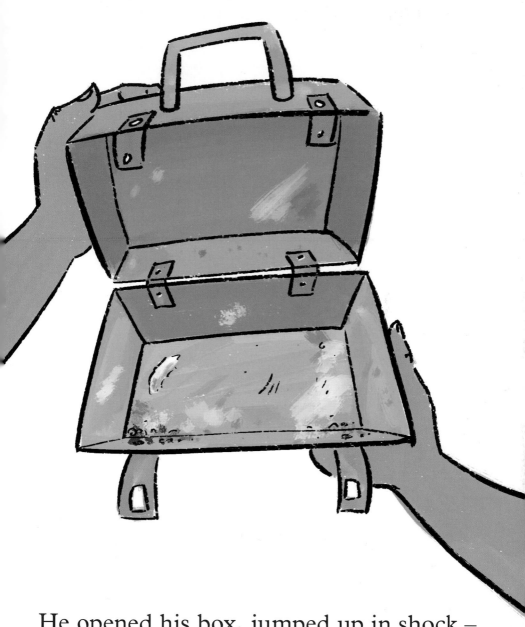

He opened his box, jumped up in shock –
His sandwiches! Nowhere in sight!

"I just have crumbs and no clue!
Someone left crumbs in my lunchbox...
But WHO?"

To his dog, Joe, he asked, "Where'd
they go?!"
And Joe gave a kind of a shrug.
Kay came along, asked what was wrong
And then gave her husband a hug.

He told her he'd made an egg
mayonnaise
A filling that filled him with glee.

And on that morning he'd stuffed a lot more in
He knew he'd be hungry, you see.

"I think," Kay said, "you have to suspect
An animal's eaten your lunch...
Probably what's best is, you turn
detective
And ask every one of the bunch!"

CRUMBS!

"I just have crumbs and no clue!
Someone left crumbs in my lunchbox...
But WHO?"

Joe stayed with Kay, while Dan
walked away
And marched himself straight to
the paddock.
Then in due course, he said to the horse,
"Harry, did you eat my sandwich?"

Harry, surprised, blinked his eyes twice,
And said, "*I eat veg and hay.*
So, what was in it? Grass or some
spinach?"
Dan told him, "Egg mayonnaise."

The horse
stamped a leg,
said, "I don't
like egg
Perhaps you
should talk to
the *hens*."

Daniel said
"sorry", continued
to worry
And went to his
feathery friends.

Bridget the chicken, corn kernel picking,
Said, "Daniel dear, don't you do *farming*?
You know eggs come from out of my *bum*
But thought I'd eat *those* did you?
Charming!"

Dan felt quite awkward so he shuffled
forward
To question a small pig called Bill.
"Why seek a grudge? You know I eat
sludge!"
Said Bill as he scoffed on his swill.

"*I just have crumbs and no clue!*
Someone left crumbs in my lunchbox…
But WHO?"

Dan rolled his eyes. A duck waddled by –
Sally, the oldest and wisest.
"Daniel, I fear it's your nearest and dearest
In life who provide the surprises."

He looked at the cows, then at the house,
"She couldn't mean Kay did it,
could she?!"

He ran like a soldier
and nearly tripped over
A goat who was napping called Woody.

He burst through the door – guess what he saw?

His wife eating! He watched her closely. *"Is that my lunch?!"* But after a crunch Kay just said, "Cheese and ham toastie."

CRUMBS!

"*I just have crumbs and no clue!*
Someone left crumbs in my lunchbox…
But WHO?"

"Sorry, I guess I'm terribly stressed,"
Said Dan as he flopped on a chair.
Then he saw one thing, the tiniest
something
That forced him to stop and to stare.

He shook as he took a look in a nook
And found bits of egg and some fur.
He glared at it there, stared at Kay's hair,
Decided the fur wasn't hers...

Then with a sniff, his bottom lip slipped,
His jaw fell incredibly low.
"Sally was *right* – the thief *was* inside.
It wasn't my wife..."

Hearing his name,
the sheepdog
exclaimed,
"Wait! You've
got it all wrong!"

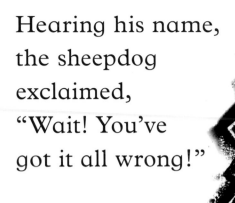

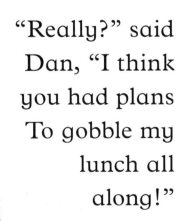

"Really?" said
Dan, "I think
you had plans
To gobble my
lunch all
along!"

"All right, okay," Joe started to say,
Most sheepish of sheepdogs around,
"You're right. I ate it, 'cause *YOU* never make it
For *ME* so I felt a bit down."

Dan said, "Who knew your favourite food
Was egg mayo? You never mentioned!"
"Maybe," said Kay, "that was Joe's way
Of trying to get your attention."

CRUMBS!

"I just had crumbs and no clue!
I should have shared my egg mayo
with you!"

Then, as Kay saw Dan shaking Joe's paw,
She knew all their troubles were through.
"One thing," she said, "a farm has is eggs.
There'll always be plenty for two!"